CrackBoom! Books is an imprint of Chouette Publishing (1987) Inc.

Text: Evelyne Fournier
Ilustrations: Chloloula
Translation: Nathaniel Penn

Chouette Publishing would like to thank the Government of Canada and SODEC for their financial support.

Canada

Québec
Books
Tax Credit
Gestion
SODEC

Bibliothèque et Archives nationales du Québec and Library and Archives Canada cataloguing in publication

Title: Mama bird lost an egg/Evelyne Fournier; illustrations, Chloloula; translation, Nathaniel Penn.

Other titles: Maman hirondelle. English

Names: Fournier, Évelyne, 1981-author. | Chloloula, 1979- illustrator. | Penn, Nathaniel, translator.

Description: Translation of: Maman hirondelle.

Identifiers: Canadiana 20190017783 | ISBN 9782898020827

Classification: LCC PS8611.O8717 M3613 2019 | DDC jC843/.6—dc23

Legal deposit – Bibliothèque et Archives nationales du Québec, 2019.
Legal deposit – Library and Archives Canada, 2019.

 BOOKS

©2019 Chouette Publishing (1987) Inc.
1001 Lenoir St., Suite B-238
Montreal, Quebec H4C 2Z6 Canada
crackboombooks.com

Printed in China
10 9 8 7 6 5 4 3 2 1 CHO2070 MAY2019

Mama Bird
LOST AN EGG

Text: Evelyne Fournier
Illustrations: Chloloula
Translation: Nathaniel Penn

CRACKBOOM!

When little Gabriel loses a feather from his wing, it's Mommy Swallow who comforts him and makes his tears take flight.

But today, Gabriel's world is turned upside down and his heart is broken. He has just discovered his mother with tears streaming down her cheeks.

Gabriel nestles in her lap. He wishes he could sing to her a comforting song, but his throat is too tight.

"There was a terrible accident last night",
Mommy tells him. "It has to do with the little egg
I've been keeping warm in the nest up there."

"The nest collapsed", Mommy Swallow explains to Gabriel, "and the egg fell. Not even the straw on the ground could slow down its senseless flight."

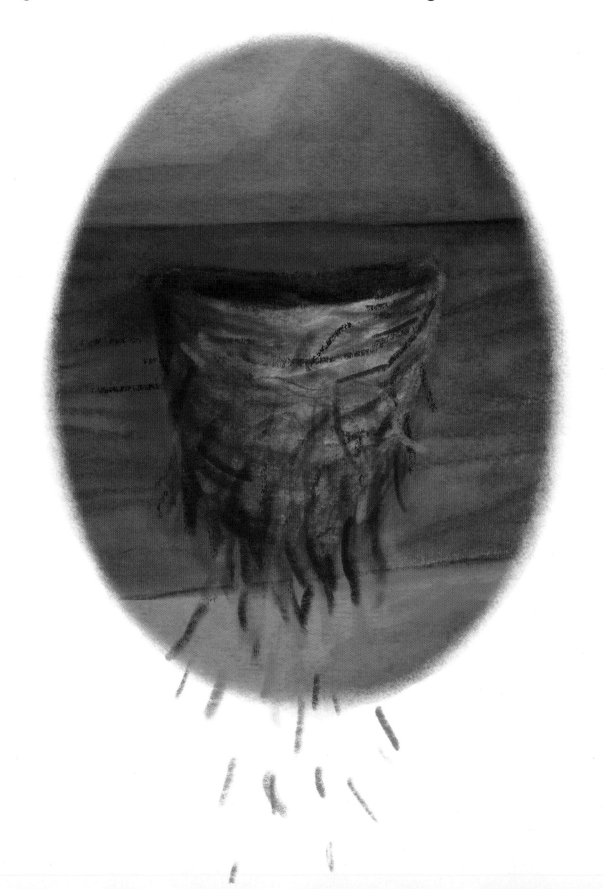

Gabriel is very sad. He had been so proud to become a big brother, but now he understands that there won't be a new chick after all.

That's when he thinks of a way
to comfort his beloved mother.
"Come with me!" he says.

Gabriel spreads his wings and rises into the sky. Curving his little chest into the wind, he invites his mother to wheel with him through the fresh summer air.

Together, they twist across the sky until they're almost out of breath.

They skim the top of a wheatfield in front of a herd of astonished cows.

They dive into streams, greeting the lovebirds.

Pausing at the very top of a great pine tree, the two swallows admire the forest in the distance. The serenity of a beautiful day surrounds them.

Their little hearts are soothed by a landscape so wonderful they might have dreamed it.

Then, as a light breeze caresses their feathers, the sun finally appears from behind the clouds.

"No one else can cheer me up like you can", Mommy says, hugging him.

Gabriel is proud of himself,
because his Mommy's eyes are
smiling again.